BRUX
THE TUSKED TERROR

With special thanks to Brandon Robshaw

For Jericho Aiken

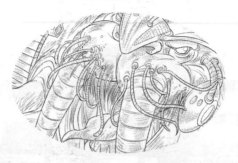

www.seaquestbooks.co.uk

ORCHARD BOOKS
338 Euston Road, London NW1 3BH
Orchard Books Australia
Level 17/207 Kent St, Sydney, NSW 2000

A Paperback Original
First published in Great Britain in 2015

Series created by Beast Quest Limited, London

Text © Beast Quest Limited 2015
Cover and inside illustrations by Artful Doodlers,
with special thanks to Bob and Justin © Orchard Books 2015

A CIP catalogue record for this book is available from
the British Library.

ISBN 978 1 40833 473 7

The paper and board used in this paperback are natural recyclable
products made from wood grown in sustainable forests. The
manufacturing processes conform to the environmental regulations of
the country of origin.

Orchard Books is a division of Hachette Children's Group, an
published by Hachette Children's Group, a division of Hachette
company.

BRUX
THE TUSKED TERROR

BY ADAM BLADE

ORCHARD

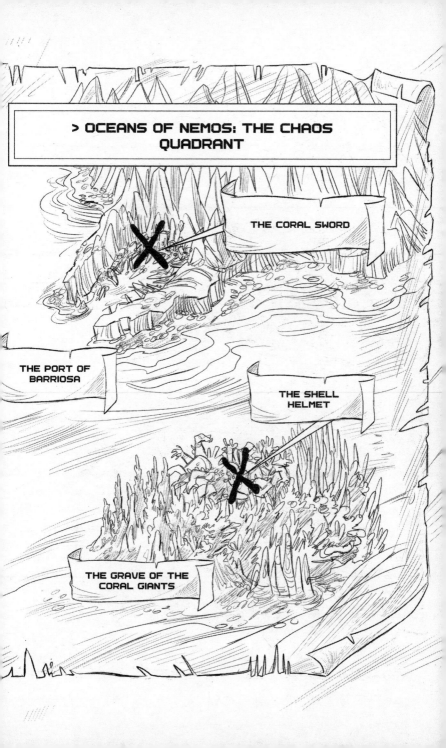

I have waited in the shadows long enough, perfecting myself. Now I will strike at my wretched enemies and make all Nemos bow before me. All I need to complete my plan are the Arms of Addulis: the Spear, the Breastplate, the Sword and the Helmet.

My mother used to tell me stories of their power, and for a long time I thought they were myths. But now I know they are real, buried in this vast ocean and waiting for a new master to wield them. With the Arms of Addulis in my control, no Merryn or human will be able to stop me.

But... I almost hope there is some pathetic hero foolish enough to try. My Robobeasts are ready — unlike anything these oceans have witnessed before. My enemies will learn that their flesh is weak.

Quake before your new leader!

RED EYE

CHAPTER ONE

ENEMY ASTERN!

Max eased back into his soft leather seat on the bridge of the *Lizard's Revenge* and gazed through the wide, smoked-glass window before him. Lia's swordfish Spike was swimming ahead, his sharp dorsal fin slicing the waves.

I could get used to this! Max thought. Especially since he felt like he'd been hit by a hover-bus from his battle with Sythid the Spider Crab. He shifted his aching body, remembering the crushing pain of being trapped in the robotic creature's claw after finding the Pearl Spear of Addulis.

Beside him, Lia was leaning against the blinking control panel that ran the width of the bridge, twirling the pearl-encrusted spear. Her Amphibio mask covered the lower part of her face, letting her breathe out of water.

She gave the spear a flick, and balanced it upright on the tip of her finger. "I still can't believe I'm holding one of the Arms of Addulis!" she said.

Roger glanced over from his seat at the wheel. "I'd say you're a natural with it lassie," he said, "but seeing as how it's powerful enough to rip a hole in my ship, maybe you could stop flinging it about?"

"Your ship?" said Lia. "I thought you said you'd 'borrowed' it." She tossed the spear into the air, then caught it deftly. "Anyway,

how far are we from the next piece of battle-gear?"

Roger pointed his hook at the holomap that Max's dogbot, Rivet, was projecting into the air before him. A big red X flickered near the position of their ship. "Well, me hearties," Roger said, "looks like it's not far at all. Which makes it strange that Red Eye's cyrates haven't shown up."

Max felt a cold finger trace his spine at the thought of the skeletal robots. He'd never seen tech so advanced. Except for the dead blankness of their glowing red eyes, the robots almost seemed alive. Each wore a black tunic with a huge scarlet eye, the symbol of the mysterious pirate who controlled them.

According to Roger, Red Eye had already taken over the Chaos Quadrant as well as the Pirate Council. And he wasn't stopping there. The spear Max and Lia had recovered was one of four pieces of legendary battle-gear that had belonged to Addulis, the first King of Sumara, who had led the ancient war between the Merryn people and humans. Red Eye was trying to get his hands on all four bits of equipment, so Max and Lia needed to get to them first.

"They won't be far behind us," Max said. "It was lucky Rivet managed to snap an image of the map while they were stealing it, otherwise we'd have no chance of beating them to the Arms of Addulis."

"Rivet good boy!" said Rivet, cheerfully.

"Bam! Bam!" Grace, Roger's niece, burst into the bridge squinting down the barrel of her toy blaster pistol. One eye was still covered with a fake eye patch to match her uncle's. "Take that, you stinking Spider Crab!" she cried, launching herself at Roger's back and grabbing him round the neck.

"Hey!" Roger cried. He pulled her over his shoulder and gave her a tickle. "Now, sea sprog, what did I tell you is the first rule of pirating?" Roger asked. He set her down on the ground, frowning. "Look out for number one! That's what," Roger went on. "No heroics. And definitely no jumping on giant Robobeasts! What'll I tell your nana if you end up as fish-food?"

Grace pouted. "Pirates aren't afraid of anything!" she said.

'Well, I'm afraid of your nana," Roger said, "so –"

BOOM! Max was almost thrown from his chair as a thunderous blast rocked the ship. Grace tumbled forwards into Roger's arms.

"Cannon fire!" Max said. Another blast shook the bridge.

Roger spun around and checked his monitors. "Company astern!" he cried.

"I'll man the guns!" Grace said, leaping towards the door.

Lia grabbed her arm. "No you won't!" she said, as Max grabbed his hyperblade and dashed out on deck.

Whoosh! A fizzing energy ball whizzed through the air and smashed down beside him, making the deck leap. Max grabbed the gunwale to keep his balance. Behind them, he could see a small, sleek ship cutting through the water. His heart raced as he saw a skull-and-crossbones fluttering from its mast. *Pirates!* And they were gaining fast.

Spike lifted his long nose out of the water.

"Spike!" Max shouted. "Get under the ship!"

Whoosh! Another energy ball fizzed towards the *Lizard's Revenge* just as Spike dipped out of sight. Max leaped aside as it smashed into the flagpole and sent it crashing onto the deck.

"Broadside them, Max!" Roger's voice cut through his headset. "We've got more guns than that one-eyed sea snail!"

"I'm already on it!" said Max. He dashed to the control panel to program the cannons that ran the length of the ship, flicked the switches that armed them, typed in the trajectory, and hit fire. The whole bank of cannons started blasting at once. A hail of golden energy balls filled the sky.

That should do it, thought Max. But just before the energy balls hit their target, they flared and vanished, leaving a faint halo around the pirate ship.

"They've got an energy shield!" Max cried.

The speeding ship was already so close he could see the crew pouring out onto the deck. There were species from all over Nemos, all armed with the latest tech. Max spotted black-eyed Gustadians, huge rock-like Grundles, even one of the tattooed monkey-like creatures from Verdula. They waved their hyperblade cutlasses and leered at him with ugly grins.

"I need backup!" Max called into his headset.

Two Gustadians were unfurling ropes over the side of their ship. "Prepare to board!" one cried.

Lia dashed out on deck holding the Pearl Spear of Addulis, Rivet close at her heels. Max grinned and lifted his hyperblade. "Let's show them what we're made of!" he said.

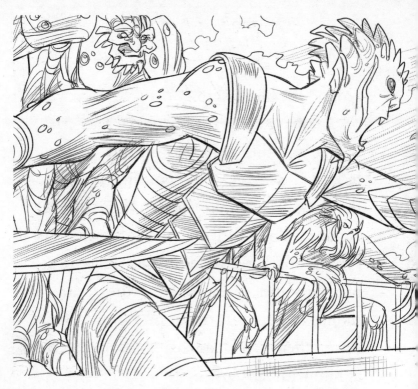

The pirates began chucking grappling
hooks, which latched onto the gunwale of
the *Lizard's Revenge*. Max scrambled to his
feet to dislodge the hooks but the pirates
were already shimmying along the ropes
towards them. The first of the pirates swung
his leg over the gunwale and leaped down
onto the deck. It was a Gustadian with a huge
puckered scar running down one cheek.

"Ha harr!" the pirate shouted, drawing his hyperblade cutlass. "Let the killin' begin!" Behind him, a wave of pirates clambered onto the deck.

CHAPTER TWO

PIRATES AHOY!

Max lunged towards the Gustadian, and their blades met with a clash that jolted along Max's arm.

The Gustadian leaped back, his long scar twitching as he grinned.

"Show us what yer got, yer scurvy dog!" the pirate shouted, starting to circle Max. Out of the corner of his eye, Max saw Lia swipe at a Grundle with the strength-enhancing Spear. The massive creature hurtled through the air and landed in the sea with a splash as Lia turned her spear on another.

Max tightened his grip on his hyperblade. "You asked for it!" he cried, slashing for the Gustadian's chest. The pirate's cutlass lashed out, swiping his blow aside.

"Is that the best you can do?" the pirate sneered, slicing his cutlass at Max's face.

Max ducked, then lunged and jabbed for the Gustadian's ribs, but the pirate twisted out of reach. Max leaped after him. He lifted his blade and brought it down with all his strength. *Take that!* Sparks flew as the pirate parried the blow, staggering under its force.

Max turned to see another pirate lunging at him.

"Ruff! Ruff!" Rivet dived forwards and clamped his teeth around the pirate's leg.

"Aargh!" The pirate toppled and landed with a grunt, but another Gustadian was already leaping over his fallen shipmate.

We've got no chance against so many! Max thought.

Suddenly Grace's voice piped up above the noise. "Prepare to get blasted, naughty pirates!" she cried, charging from the bridge wearing her deepsuit and jet-powered boots. She waved her blaster. *Oh no!* Max thought.

Roger appeared, red-faced and panting.

"Grace! Get back here right now!" he shouted. But Grace fired the underwater thrusters on her boots and whooshed up into the air.

"Ha ha!" she cried, zooming over Max's head. She smashed into the Gustadian's shoulders, knocking him to the floor.

Max ran forward, but pirates swarmed in from every direction, blocking his path.

"Get off me, you slimy lizard!" Grace shouted. A broad pirate with a scaly face framed by frills had lifted her off the ground. *A Kroy!* Max had met Kroy before, in the Forest of Souls. But this one had a skull-and-crossbones tattoo on his neck, partly covered by a small metal box with a blinking red light. *Could he be another of Red Eye's robotic creations?* Max wondered with a jolt. Grace was kicking frantically in the Kroy's arms.

"Stop yer wriggling, yer little scoundrel," the Kroy shouted, pressing the muzzle of his blaster to her head. "Avast, lads!" he called to the pirates. "I think we've made our point!"

The pirates lowered their weapons.

"I'm Captain Rung'alal," the Kroy pirate cried, "famed pirate of the Chaos Quadrant. If you want this spratling back in one piece, you'd better do as I say."

Roger hurried forwards, his hands raised.

"No need for that, matey," he said. "We're all pirates here –"

"Enough o' yer rubbish!" Rung'alal interrupted. "Ye're no pirate! Yer too lily-livered to defend yer own ship. Or should I say *my* ship, which you stole from me."

Roger winced. "It was empty," he said. "Fair plunder! What's a pirate to do?"

"Of course we nicked it!" Grace shouted, squirming in the Kroy's arms. "We're pirates!"

"We only left it to celebrate stealing Elrith's map off a blind old Merryn woman in Astar," Rung'alal said. "We weren't expecting some barnacle-faced puke-bucket to go swiping it from under our noses."

Max frowned. *Is every pirate in the Chaos Quadrant after that map?*

Lia stepped forward, her face red with anger. "You had no right to take that map!" she shouted in fury.

"Why did you want it?" Max asked.

The Kroy suddenly looked uncomfortable. He shifted his feet, then spat angrily at the ground. "Cos Red Eye made us, that's why. If we don't get that map to him sharpish we're all dead. And he'll be after you too. Nothin' stands in his path."

"We're not scared of stupid Red Eye!" Grace shouted.

"Well, you should be," Rung'alal said. "He's not like other pirates. He don't follow the pirate code. He don't even care for grog and sea shanties. Look." The pirate tapped the metal box on his neck. "You know what this is?" he asked. "It's a bomb. Red Eye put it there, and unless I get that map to him soon, it's goin' to blow. So you better give it me now, if you know what's good for yer."

Max and Lia exchanged an uneasy glance. "We don't have the map," Max said.

"What do you mean you don't have it?" the Kroy captain shouted, his eyes bulging.

"Red Eye has it," Max said. "His cyrates stole it."

The frills around the captain's cheeks started to quiver. The hand holding the blaster to Grace's head twitched alarmingly.

"Don't squeeze me so tight!" Grace shouted.

Max's eyes fell on the box attached to Rung'alal's neck, and suddenly, he had an idea. "Look," Max said, "I'll disarm the bomb for you in exchange for Grace and the ship."

Rung'alal gaped at Max. "If you think I'll let a landlubber like you touch it you're a lobster short of a catch," he said.

"No, really," said Max. "I'm great with tech. I can fix anything. I made my robodog from scratch." He pointed at Rivet, who wagged his tail cheerfully.

Captain Rung'alal narrowed his eyes. "All right," he said finally, "but one false move, and the sprog gets it. Thrasher! Catch!" Grace squeaked as the pirate captain tossed her into the long, hairy arms of the monkey-like Verdulan pirate. The Verdulan tucked Grace under his arm and grinned, baring pointed teeth.

"Get on with it then!" Rung'alal said. "But remember, it ain't just me you're messing with. You get this wrong and everyone on board will be blown to smithereens."

Max breathed out and moved forward. The box on the captain's neck was sleek and silver without a crack or opening in sight.

Max thought of Red Eye's cyrates, and his hands grew slick with sweat.

If the bomb's as advanced as they are, we're in trouble!

CHAPTER THREE

ONE FALSE MOVE

"Right," Max said, looking at the bomb on Rung'alal's scaly neck. "If you could just...crouch down a bit?" The captain scowled, but dropped to one knee. Max bent over him, trying to ignore the unwashed piratey stink.

He ran his fingers over the smooth lines of the box, looking for any markings. Stamped into the side he could see a manufacturer's symbol. *Siborg*, Max read. He continued his

search. *Aha!* He could feel the faint lines
of a hidden panel. He held his breath as he
pressed the edge of it. *This had better not be
a trap…* But the hatch flicked open to reveal
an intricate pattern of transparent tubes,
and a screen with a flashing red light. Max's
heart sank. *I've never seen anything like this!*

He wiped his sweaty hands and reached

inside the box. As soon as the tip of his finger touched one of the tubes, the whole box buzzed. Max snatched his hand away.

"Wossat?" the Kroy snapped.

"Nothing," Max said. But then he noticed a red light forming numbers. *10, 9, 8…*

Oh no! Max's mouth went dry. *It's going to blow!*

His mind raced. There wasn't time to disarm it. *I'll have to take it off!* He felt along the rough scales of Rung'alal's neck for the mechanism that fastened the box.

7, 6, 5…

No time! Only one thing left to try…

Max took a step back and whipped out his hyperblade.

"What are yer doing?" Rung'alal said, his gruff voice quavering.

Max didn't answer. He lifted his hyperblade. *Swish!* He brought it down where the box attached to the pirate's neck. The thin blade sliced through the connecting wires. Max flicked his blade, flinging the bomb over the gunwale. He held his breath as the bomb hit the water with a splash.

Boom! An enormous wave surged over the ship, soaking them all. Max shook himself, and let out a shuddering sigh. *That was close.*

Rung'alal rubbed his neck. "Am I glad to get that cursed bit o' tech off!" he said. "Much obliged, matey!" He turned to the pirate holding Grace. "Let the tiddler go," he said.

The long-armed Verdulan set Grace down. Immediately she swung around and stamped hard on his hairy foot.

"Eeeeoooooagggghhhh!" he screeched.

"Hey! No cursin' in front of the sprog!" Rung'alal shouted. Roger grabbed Grace by the arm and dragged her towards the bridge.

Max turned to Rung'alal. "That was one

scary bit of tech you were wearing," he said. "More advanced than anything I've seen. What do you know about Red Eye?"

Rung'alal swallowed hard. "Not much, if truth be told," he said. "His real name's Siborg, but I couldn't tell you what he looks like. He sends those filthy cyrates to do his biddin'. Speaks through 'em too. Sent a chill right down my spine when one of those robots started talking. As far as I can tell, Red Eye's bent on taking over the whole o' Delta Quadrant. Sumara too." Rung'alal nodded towards Lia. "Then, who knows? The whole of Nemos, probably. You'd do well to get yer hides as far away as you can, just like I'm going to do." Rung'alal turned to his crew. "Lads!" he shouted. "Make ready! We're getting out o' here."

Max stiffened and put his hand on the hilt of his blade. "We need this ship," he said.

Rung'alal gave a bark of laughter. "Don't worry, lad," he said. "Yer welcome to her. Red Eye'll be tracking her, I reckon, and I'm not planning on being here when he finds her!"

Max watched as the pirates shimmied back along their grappling lines to their new ship. Then he and Lia unhitched the hooks and tossed them overboard before making their way back to the bridge, followed by Rivet.

They found Grace grinning and rubbing her little hands together. "Good riddance to bad rubbish!" she said.

"You were lucky Max is handy with tech," Roger said from his seat at the wheel. "Keep yer head below deck next time!" Roger flipped a lever, and Max felt the ship start to move. Obediently, Rivet projected the map for the pirate to navigate.

"Let's hope there isn't a next time," Lia muttered, gazing out to sea.

Max frowned. "With Red Eye and his cyrates tracking the next of the Arms of Addulis, there's not much chance of that," he said. Lia put her fingers to her temples. Max realised she was using her Aqua Powers. "How's Spike?" he asked.

Lia blinked and turned. "He's fine," she said. "He was swept away by the force of the bomb, but he's on his way back to us now."

"Phew!" Max said. "That was one serious explosion. And it's got me worried. With that sort of tech, if Red Eye gets any of the Arms of Addulis too, he'll be unstoppable."

"He won't," Grace said, "because we'll get there first!"

"We'll have to," Max said. "Lia? Rung'alal called the map Elrith's Map. Do you know what he meant?"

Lia frowned. "Elrith was Addulis's councillor," she said. "He must have hidden the Arms, then made the map in Astar. It's just a village outside Sumara. So how could Red Eye have known where to look?"

Max shook his head. "He always seems one step ahead. And after our run-in with those pirates, he's probably beaten us to the next mark on the map. I expect we'll find one of his Robobeasts waiting for us."

"We'll see soon enough," Roger said. "But in the meantime, I could do with an extra pair of eyes keeping a lookout."

"Aye aye, Captain," Max said, joining Roger at the controls. Lia and Grace came too, and Rivet sat beside Max.

The sea was choppy and grey, and as Max watched, mist began to rise. Max strained his eyes, staring into the fog, but he couldn't see more than a ship's length ahead.

"Just what we need!" Max said. "There could be cyrates anywhere. We won't see them coming in this!"

"We're headed towards the Lost Caves of Chi," Roger said. "It ain't going to be pretty. Earthquakes…storms…currents. Not to mention all the ghosts." Roger gave the wheel a sharp tug, veering past a jagged rock.

"Ghosts?" Grace said nervously.

"Aye," Roger said. "That's what they say. More ships have been wrecked on these rocks than I can count. The mists come up, the currents change…and *bam*. Legend has it that drowned men haunt these waters, hungry for company."

Max stared out into the mist. Ghosts. Looking into the eerie shifting greyness ahead, he could almost believe it. There was an electric tingle in the air that set his nerves on edge, making the skin on his scalp creep.

Someone or something was watching. He could feel it.

CHAPTER FOUR

GHOST IN THE DEEP

As the *Lizard's Revenge* glided through curling tendrils of mist, the crawling feeling on Max's skin got steadily worse. At the wheel, Roger was wiping sweat from his forehead as he steered sharply between rocks and other dark shapes that looked like partly sunken wrecks. Lia, Max, Grace and Rivet all sat in silence, watching as the shadowy forms swept past.

Sometimes the water around the ship was

choppy and white with foam. Other times it was a flat, dirty blue with a faint shimmer of colours on the surface.

"Look," Max said, pointing to the sheen on the water. "That must be fuel from sunken boats."

A great metallic thud rocked the ship, the sound echoing around them.

"Is that the ghosts?" Grace asked, her voice quavering with excitement.

"Earthquakes, more likely," Roger whispered, "but truth is, there's no telling what's out there."

Max rubbed the back of his neck, trying to get rid of the prickling feeling.

Lia shifted her shoulders. "I can sense it

too, Max," she said. "Like someone's watching us."

"Look out!" Grace cried, pointing through the window. Roger wrenched the wheel as a huge shape loomed before them, twice as high as the ship. The *Lizard's Revenge* wheeled sharply, and Max slid sideways as a colossal wreck slid past. Tattered sails billowed in the mist and dark holes gaped in the ship's barnacle-encrusted sides.

"Whoa! She's a beauty!" Roger breathed.

"Ghost, Max!" Rivet barked, staring at the ship.

Max followed Rivet's gaze, and spotted a glimmer of red. *There!* Deep in the shadows on the deck of the ship, a red light glinted. As Max watched, it blinked and went out. In its place Max thought he saw the shadowy lines of a dark figure slip into the shadows. It could have been a trick of the light, or it could have been a cyrate. But the shape had moved more like a person...

I'm not taking any chances, Max thought.

"I'm going to scout ahead in my hydrodisk," Max said to the others. "Make sure the coast is clear."

"I'll come too," Lia said.

"And me!" Grace chimed in.

"No you won't," Roger said, clamping a hand down on his niece's shoulder. "We'll anchor here. You can help me keep a lookout until Max and Lia give the all clear." Grace scowled but stayed in her seat.

Max and Lia headed up on deck, with Rivet trotting at their heels. Thick mist gusted against them in chilly sheets, and a fine rain prickled Max's skin. Somewhere far below Max could hear the hollow creak of metal grating on metal in the depths.

Lia climbed onto the gunwale. "I'll meet

you down there," she said. She flicked back her silver hair, and dived into the oily water. Max watched her surface with Spike. She waved, then ducked back under.

Max climbed through a hatch on deck and descended the stairs to the belly of the ship, where his hydrodisk waited.

As the sight of the smooth, sleek lines of his sub, Max felt a twinge of excitement.

He flipped open the cockpit and slipped into the pilot's seat, running his hands over the shining controls. He put on his headset, then touched a button. The hydrodisk whirred into life. The cockpit closed smoothly as the airlock behind Max slid shut. The hatch of the *Lizard's Revenge* opened revealing the surface of the ocean. The metal runners underneath the hydrodisk tilted, sending the sub sliding into the water. Max flicked on his headlamps, gunned the engines and shot out into the depths.

The sub cast two bright columns of light into the murky water ahead. Max stared about in awe. Far below, the ocean floor was rutted with deep cracks and chasms. From the depths rose great columns of rock. Some reached all the way to the surface, while others held the battered, barnacle-encrusted

remains of sunken vessels, spilling streams of oil into the sea.

Max spotted Lia surging towards him on Spike, and Rivet swam in the swordfish's wake. Lia grimaced and coughed as they pulled up alongside him.

"This water is disgusting!" she said into her headset.

"It's no wonder," Max said. "It looks like a ships' graveyard down here!" He heard a whirr of propellers from above, and looked up to see Rivet speeding towards him.

"Smelly water, Max," Rivet said.

Lia coughed again. "Let's go," she said. "The quicker we're out of this oil slick the better. Come on, Spike." Her swordfish flicked his tail and shot forwards. Max hit the accelerator, feeling a rush of speed as he darted after Lia. Rivet's propellers hummed as he whizzed along beside them.

Max swerved between towers of rock. Pale fish with dark, empty eyes swept past the hydrodisk.

He rounded a column, pushing through the tattered remains of a skeletal ship's sails.

Whoa! Max slammed on his brakes and jolted to a stop. Lia and Rivet stopped beside him. Ahead of them, a great wall of bronze blocked the way.

"What's that?" Lia said. Max stared. It was immense. It looked like a sunken tanker, floating just below the surface.

But the more he looked, the less like a tanker it seemed. It was curved, like a bloated torpedo. And the metal seemed to move in and out. Almost like it was breathing…

"Lia! Get back!" Max shouted, just as the metal wall before him buckled and curved in on itself. Max found himself looking into black, red-rimmed eyes either side of a hairy snout. Two huge tusks, each the size of an aquabike, jutted down from the creature's face. *A walrus?* Max thought. But it was enormous. And definitely robotically altered. Its bronze-plated belly looked broad enough to crush a ship. Stamped onto the creature's gigantic breastplate was a single word. *Brux.* Max recognised the writing from the name

on Rung'alal's bomb. *Siborg. AKA Red Eye.*

Max slammed his hydrodisk into reverse, aiming his blasters at the huge Robobeast.

"It's a trap," Lia cried from beside him. She pointed into the murky water beyond Brux. A swarm of skeletal cyrates darted from behind the creature, their red eyes bright in the gloom. Max saw that instead of feet, they

had metallic flippers, almost like Merryn feet. *Siborg must have upgraded them!* Max realised.

He swivelled the aim of his blasters to focus on the cyrates. But, before he could fire, Brux flexed his huge, metal-clad body and sent his massive tail swiping towards him.

Max braced himself. There was a moment of stillness. Then the current of water hit. Max's head was thrown backwards as the hydrodisk surged off, spinning around and around. He heard Lia screaming, mixed with the swooshing sound of water. He gripped his joystick, trying to bring the spinning hydrodisk under control. Bubbles and sediment streamed past. He caught a glimpse of Lia, gripping Spike's back tightly as they were swept away.

A moment later he saw the rusted hulk of a sunken ship rushing towards him. A wall of solid metal. Max's stomach lurched. He wrenched his joystick, trying to turn. But the current was too strong. He clenched his teeth and braced his muscles. *I'm going to crash!*

CHAPTER FIVE

A SITTING DUCK

CLANG! The hollow sound of metal on metal rang in Max's ears as he was catapulted forward. His shoulder slammed against the roof of his hydrodisk. Then his hip smashed into the floor. There was a metallic scraping sound and then everything went still. Max scrambled up, his head cloudy and his shoulder throbbing with pain. He slid into his seat and fumbled with the controls, hurriedly checking the displays. *Thank goodness!* Everything seemed to be working.

He glanced through the watershield, but all he could see was the crumpled metal of the wreck.

Max pulled on his headset. "Lia," he called, "are you and Spike okay?"

"Just bruised," Lia replied. "How about you?"

"The same. Can you see Rivet?"

"I can't see a thing. The water's too dirty!" said Lia.

Max felt a pang of worry for his dogbot, but with a Robobeast and a gang of cyrates on the loose, they couldn't look for him now.

"We'll find him later," Max said. "Right now, it's time to blast some robo-backside!" He threw the hydrodisk into reverse, then swung it around and flipped it into forward gear. Spike and Lia swooped into view. Max grinned.

"Ready?" he said. Lia nodded. Max flicked

a switch, arming the hydrodisk's torpedoes. He scanned the cloudy water. *Where's that monstrous walrus?*

But all he could see were the shadowy shapes of rocks and sunken ships. There was no sign of the huge bronze monster. Then Max noticed a collection of small red points up ahead. He swung his headlamps towards them. The skeletal forms of at least twenty cyrates hung in the water, their red eyes glowing.

"Lia!" Max said. "Get below the sub! I'm going to zap those cyrates." He tapped in a command, setting his blasters to rapid fire. *They won't know what's hit them!* Max lifted his finger to hit *fire*…

A strange, static vibration washed over him. It made the hair on his arms stand on end. The sub's engines went silent, and the lights flickered and went out. Max hit the power button, and tugged at the control stick. Nothing. The sub was dead. Max felt a stab of alarm. He tried hitting *fire* again. Still nothing.

The cyrates were drawing closer, their blasters aimed and ready. Max jabbed at buttons and flicked switches, his palms slick with sweat. *I'm a sitting duck.*

Suddenly, Lia let out a harsh battle cry and swooped from beneath the sub. She lifted the Pearl Spear of Addulis and charged towards the cyrates on Spike. Max felt a wave of relief. *Go, Lia!*

The cyrates opened fire. Red energy beams streaked through the water. As Spike and Lia dodged between them, Lia swiped out with her spear, slicing a cyrate clean in half.

Max flung the hatch to the hydrodisk's airlock open, then exited the sub. He drew the water over his gills, thanking the Merryn

Touch that let him breathe underwater. He pulled his blaster from his belt.

Cyrates were scattering, darting away from Lia's spear. Max kicked back hard, powering himself forwards. As he surged at the cyrates, he fired his blaster over and over.

Red energy bolts sizzled past him as the cyrates returned fire. Max twisted his body and flicked his legs, dodging right, then left, out of their deadly path.

Up ahead, Lia and Spike were zigzagging as Lia lashed out with her spear, smashing arms and legs off the skeletal black robots. Max's shots were taking their toll too. He watched with satisfaction as one blast hit a cyrate's chest, and its glowing eyes went dark.

Suddenly, as if they'd heard a signal, the cyrates darted away into the shadow of a rocky ledge. *They're regrouping*, Max realised. All at once the cyrates reappeared in close formation. They started advancing, red eyes flashing steadily. The whole ocean seemed to glow red as the cyrates opened fire.

Lia dived out of range behind a craggy column of rock, and Max kicked hard, racing to join her. Max slammed his back against the rock, his heart racing.

He peered out at the line of cyrates and his stomach churned. *There are way too many of them.*

"What now?" Lia asked.

"Hold on, Maxy boy!" Roger's voice blurted though Max's headset. "We're on our way!" Roger and Grace plunged into the water behind the cyrates, their deepsuits trailing bubbles. Max let out a whoop of relief. Grace and Roger were holding blaster cannons; Grace's weapon was longer than her arm! They fired together, sending huge energy blasts towards the cyrates. Bits of black metal exploded in every direction, and the flippers of the remaining cyrates flicked as they darted away. Roger and Grace surged after them, firing into the group from either side.

Max hurled himself out from behind his

rock and opened fire, taking out a pair of retreating robots. Roger and Grace shot over and over, blasting cyrates into dust. Soon the water was filled with bits of floating robot. Max scanned the scene for more red eyes. He could see skinny robotic arms and legs trailing wires. He even spotted a robot head,

but its eyes were dead and black.

"Max!" Lia screamed. Max turned to see a cyrate powering towards him, its blaster aimed at his head. He started to lift his weapon, but there wasn't time.

I'm going to be hit!

CHAPTER SIX

STOLEN TREASURE

Max tensed his body, waiting for the inevitable pain.

Instead, something silver whizzed past him with a growl. Suddenly the cyrate was flying backwards, smashed aside by a powerful blow from Rivet's metal head. The robot's red eyes flickered and went black. Max let out a long shaky breath as Rivet zoomed towards him, tail wagging.

"Good boy!" Max said, patting his dogbot's

head. "I was worried about you!"

"Sorry," Rivet said. "I was scouting ahead. Land is not far."

Max frowned. Rivet sounded strange – kind of formal. *He's using full sentences! Maybe his vocab circuit got scrambled when Brux sent us flying.*

"Wahoo!" Grace cried, interrupting his thoughts. She did a twirl in the water. "We smashed those naughty cyrates!"

Roger grinned and ruffled her hair. "Right, me hearties," he said. "We'd better get out of here before more cyrates turn up."

"Or that Robobeast," Lia added, glancing about uneasily. Max looked at his broken hydrodisk, lying on the ocean bed.

"Roger, can you lower a net for my sub?" he asked.

"Will do, Max," Roger said. "Come on, Grace, you can give me a hand."

Roger and Grace swam up to the surface, and Rivet and Lia followed.

Left on his own, Max felt the sea around him becoming colder and darker. He glanced at the wrecked vessels, looking for any sign of Brux.

"Here it comes, Maxy boy!" Max heard Roger's voice through his headset, and looked up to see a net sinking towards him. Max grabbed it and tugged it down to the damaged sub. He wrapped it over the hydrodisk, and pulled it tight.

"Ready to go, Roger!" Max called. The net went taut, and the hydrodisk started to rise as the *Lizard's Revenge* winched it in. Max swam behind the sub, guiding it up through the water towards the ship. The airlock opened. As Max pushed the hydrodisk inside, its lights flickered and came on. Max peered through the sub's window, frowning.

The main display didn't show any alarms. *That's strange... It seems to be working fine now!*

Max waited for the water to pump out of the airlock, then tugged the net off and jumped inside the hydrodisk. He tapped in a code to run a diagnostic check. All clear. *Maybe crashing into that wreck caused a temporary glitch?* But the sub had seemed fine right after...

Max racked his brains as he took the lift to the upper deck. *Could something in the water have interfered with the sub?*

As he entered the bridge he saw right away that the mist had cleared. Sun was streaming through the windows. Craggy rocks and the wreckage of ships cast long shadows onto the oily water ahead. Beyond that, Max could see a wall of black stone rising from the ocean, pitted with caves.

"Land ahoy!" Roger cried. Grace was seated at his side while Lia was standing, gazing out over the waves.

"Any sign of Brux?" Max asked, as Roger steered the ship between the wrecks.

"Not so far," Lia said. "Spike says the ocean's deserted."

"Ha ha! We've scared Red Eye off!" Grace cried in delight.

"Somehow I doubt it," Max said. "He's probably gone after the next piece of battle-gear."

"That'd be just our luck," Roger said, easing the ship into a narrow cove of black volcanic rock. He flicked a switch, and Max heard the whir of the ship's anchor dropping.

They headed out onto the deck. The black sand of the cove crunched under Max's boots as he jumped off the ship's ladder.

Roger, Lia and Grace followed him onto the beach. A cleft ran between the cliffs, making a broad pathway inland. Max recognised the layout from Rivet's map.

"The next piece of armour should be fifty paces that way," Max said, pointing towards the cleft.

"Max…" Roger said, his voice low. "I think you should see this." Max turned to see Roger pointing out to sea, and felt a prickle of alarm.

As far as the eye could see in every
direction, the ocean was strewn with
columns of rock and the decaying wrecks
of boats. All except for a wide belt of water
leading towards them. It looked as if the
jutting rocks had been toppled and broken,
and the shipwrecks pushed aside.

*A path made by some kind of ship. Or by
some kind of enormous creature...*

"Brux!" Max said. "He must have come ashore ahead of us."

Roger let out a long whistle. "He's got to be built like a battering ram!"

"At least he should be easy to spot," Lia said. She turned to Spike, who was swimming by the side of the ship. "Spike, stay here. Warn me if Brux comes this way. We'll go and look for the armour."

"I'll come with you, Max, if that is all right," Rivet said.

Max stared at Rivet, surprised again by his strange new voice. But the dogbot was wagging his tail with his metal tongue lolling, looking just like his normal self. Max nodded, then led the way inland across the barren landscape. He couldn't see any sign of Brux or the cyrates. In fact, there wasn't a single plant or animal in sight, just high black cliffs and sharp rocks jutting from the sand like rotten teeth.

When Max had counted fifty paces, he stopped. He was facing a small rocky outcrop, with a lower ridge of rock running in front of it. He bent and looked behind the ridge. There was a hollow in the rock, and inside Max could see a blue chest covered in gold studwork.

Lia's hair fell in a curtain as she leaned over beside him. "That's a Sumaran design," she said.

Max reached down and lifted the chest up onto the ridge.

"Let me see!" Grace cried, as she and Roger hurried to join them.

"Lia, you should open it," Max said. He craned forward to look inside as she lifted the lid. At once his heart sank. *Empty!*

"Someone's stolen our treasure!" Grace cried, her uncovered eye narrowed to just

an angry slit.

"Red Eye!" Lia said.

"Or pirates," Max said, thinking of all the wrecked ships. "It could have been taken years ago."

"So, what now then?" Roger said. Max bit his lip, thinking. *We have to find that battle-gear. But it could be anywhere!*

ROOOOAR!! A thunderous cry echoed off the rock around them. It was so deep Max could feel it vibrating inside his lungs. He turned to see a mountainous, bronze-clad shape emerging from between the cliffs.

Brux!

CHAPTER SEVEN

A RACE AGAINST DEATH

The walrus's red-rimmed eyes peered at them from under wrinkled lids. The creature let out another mighty roar, then lifted its flippered tail and brought it down with an earth-shaking crash.

Max staggered as a tremendous shockwave jolted through his legs. Grace screamed and Roger grabbed her to stop her falling. Brux lifted his battering ram of a head, opened his mouth and let out another roar. The ground

shook again and rocks rained down as the
cry rumbled on.

"Roger! Take Grace back to the ship," Max
shouted. "Lia and I will handle this!"

"No way!" Grace cried. But Roger scooped
up his niece and ran.

Brux's roar finally came to an end. The

metal-clad giant heaved itself forwards, covering the ground with terrifying speed. Then it stopped and lifted its massive tail. Max braced himself as the tail plunged downwards.

Max's legs were thrown out from under him as the ground jolted. Black sand and sharp rock bit into his hands and knees as he fell. He scrambled up, dizzy.

Beside him Lia was rubbing at a gash on her elbow and Rivet was clambering to his feet. Brux was moving again, heaving itself along with his muscular flippers. Its copper-plated belly grated over the ground, crushing the rocks in its path.

"We have to disable its control box," Max said. "Can you see it?"

"There's so much metal!" Lia said. "It's hard to know where to start."

Max scanned the enormous walrus,

looking for a telltale glint of silver. Its giant armoured body reflected the sun, and its metallic tusks glinted. It raised its flat nose and looked about, whiskers quivering. As it turned, Max caught a glimpse of something small and shining behind a curved tusk. *A metal box.*

"There!" Max said, pointing.

Lia frowned. "We can't hit that with the spear like we did with Sythid," she said. "We'd have to be underneath its head."

"It would crush us in seconds!" Max said, watching as a huge rock splintered to dust under Brux's colossal weight. *It's as if Siborg knows how we defeated Sythid. And now he's put Brux's controls where we can't reach them...*

"We'll need a different plan this time," said Max. "One which starts with running. Now!"

Max turned and darted away. Rivet and Lia

pounded over the black rock behind him. The harsh sound of Brux's bronze belly sliding over the ground was almost deafening.

"We need to lead it away from the ship!" Max shouted.

They raced between the cliffs and onto the beach, heading away from the *Lizard's Revenge*. Max glanced behind him. The Robobeast was almost on them, its eyes flashing with triumph.

"Run!" Max shouted, forcing his legs to go faster. Rivet bounded beside him and Max could hear Lia's breath coming hard and fast through her Amphibio mask. His own lungs were burning, but they had to reach the water before they were crushed.

Almost there! A shadow fell over them and Max glanced back. *Whoa!* Brux was right behind them, its huge metal chest rearing skywards as it lunged.

"Into the water!" Max cried. "It's on us!" Max leaped into the waves, fear pumping through his veins. He powered downwards as fast as he could. Beside him Rivet's propellers whirred. Lia streaked ahead, gliding towards deeper water.

Max heard a tremendous splash, and a moment later a surge of water hit him, pushing him forwards. He looked back to see Brux's massive head driving towards them.

"This way!" Lia said, flicking her legs and darting between the rusting hulks of two ships. "We'll lose him among the wrecks!"

Max and Rivet swam after her, through a narrow channel between the barnacle-encrusted ships. *That brute won't fit through here!* Max thought. But then he heard a terrific metallic groaning behind him. He glanced back to see Brux ploughing straight ahead, using his metal-plated chest to smash a path

through the ships. Subs and tankers buckled and twisted as Brux forged ahead. *They're not slowing him at all.*

Max swam after Lia as fast as he could. His legs and arms flew through the water but he couldn't keep up. Ahead, he saw a flash of glistening silver. It was Spike, darting through the water towards Lia. Lia swung herself up onto her swordfish's back.

"Max!" Lia called as she surged further ahead. "Hurry!"

"I am hurrying!" Max shouted. Rivet turned in the water, his red eyes flashing.

"Max! Hold onto me!" Rivet barked, hanging back so Max could catch up. Max put his arms around Rivet's metal waist, and the dogbot's propellers hummed.

The next moment Rivet shot forwards, accelerating so fast Max's stomach felt left behind. Max held tight as shipwrecks whizzed past in a blur of speed.

Brux's angry roar filled the water behind them. Max glanced back, and his stomach clenched with fear. Brux was drawing back his massive tail, aiming it at a huge, rusted sub.

BOOM! The metallic sound of Brux's tail

hitting the sub echoed through the water and the sub shot upwards, hurtling towards them at deadly speed.

CHAPTER EIGHT

A BONE-CRUSHING FALL

"Behind those rocks!" Lia shouted from ahead, pointing to a towering formation to their left. Spike flicked his fins and darted behind it.

"Full throttle, Riv!" Max shouted, kicking his legs hard to add his power to Rivet's. The dogbot's propellers whined as he put on a burst of speed.

Max saw Lia watching from behind the rock, her eyes wide with terror. Max's heart thundered as the shadow of the huge sub fell across him, plunging him into darkness. *Almost there!* The rock was just a kick away. *Yes!* Rivet and Max dived behind it.

The sound of the sub's impact exploded around them. Bits of metal and smashed rock drifted down toward the seabed.

"Stay hidden!" Max cried. A huge shadow was emerging from the floating dust. Brux. Max flattened his back to the rock behind him, keeping out of sight. Lia did the same. The massive bronze-clad form of Brux powered past them, and Max watched as the huge walrus disappeared into the water ahead.

"That was close!" Lia said.

Max's heart was still hammering. "A bit too close," he said.

Rivet's ears pricked up. "Max, look at the spear," he said, in his strange new voice.

Lia held up the Pearl Spear of Addulis and gasped. It was glowing with a pale green light.

Max frowned. "That's what happened when the different parts of the Skull of Thallos were close to each other," he said.

Lia nodded. "It's some kind of ancient Merryn power. We must be close to the next piece of Addulis's battle-gear. The spear should show us the way."

Lia turned the spear sideways and laid it flat in the water, then slowly removed her hand. The spear floated. Then it began to move.

Max watched as it spun like a compass needle until it was pointing roughly ahead. Then it tipped, angling steeply towards the seabed, and hung in the water like an arrow.

Below them, in the dark blue water near the ocean bed, lay an ancient-looking wreck. The spear was pointing right at it. The huge rusting hulk lay on its side, teetering on the edge of a long black gash in the ocean floor. A chasm.

"Do you think the armour is in that ship?" Max asked.

"It must be," Lia said, plucking the spear

from the water.

"So, pirates must have found the armour, then been wrecked," Max said. He scanned the waters all around them, looking for any sign of Brux. He could see the flickering lights of jellyfish and a few other fish, but that was all. "Let's go," Max said. He dived downwards, Rivet, Spike and Lia swimming at his side.

They swam past ugly, scarred fish with jagged teeth. Soon Max could make out the details of the wreck. It had twisted metal railings and ladders covered in pale, straggly sea moss.

Lia slipped from Spike's back and darted towards a porthole in the upturned side of the ship.

"Rivet, stay here with Spike," Max told his dogbot. "Keep a lookout for Brux."

"Right, Max!" Rivet said. Max glanced at

the deep chasm beside the ship, but even with his underwater vision, enhanced by the Merryn Touch, he could see nothing but craggy rocks and darkness. An icy chill seemed to creep out of the blackness, prickling his skin with goose bumps.

Lia vanished through the porthole, and Max swam in after her.

Inside, the girders around the ship's hull looked like the ribs of a giant whale. Ladders ran horizontally and there were doors where windows should be. Everything was on its side, covered in barnacles and silt. Lia's spear was shining like a green lamp. It pointed downwards towards a pile of furniture resting on what had once been a wall. Lia swam down and started rummaging in the pile.

"Brux!" Rivet barked suddenly from outside. Max darted up out of the porthole to take a look. In the distance, he could see a vast, dark torpedo-like shape edging towards them.

The giant walrus was still a way off, but it was moving fast. As Max watched, the giant creature turned side on, and swished its tail through the water.

A moment later, the current hit Max like a blow. The ship below him shuddered. A terrible scraping sound echoed through its metal, and the whole thing shifted and tipped, balancing on the lip of the chasm. *He's going to push it over the edge!*

"Lia!" Max called through the porthole, "Hurry! Brux is –" The ship groaned and shuddered again as another shockwave hit. Max saw it list downwards then sway back like a giant seesaw.

"I've found it!" Lia cried. Max looked down through the porthole to see her holding up a

slab of silvery stone covered in swirling lines.
Addulis's Breastplate!

A drum-like boom echoed around them and the ship tipped suddenly downward again. Lia's eyes went wide with fear.

"Get out!" Max shouted, grabbing the edges of the porthole. The ship started to slide away, dragging him with it.

"Ahhh!" Lia cried.

"You have to get out now!" Max shouted. "The ship's falling into the chasm!"

Lia shook her head. "I can't!" she said. "I'm trapped!" Max saw that one of her legs was wedged under a chest that had fallen when the ship tipped.

"Danger, Max!" Rivet barked, while Spike let out a volley of frantic warning clicks.

Suddenly the ship jerked away from Max, almost ripping his arms from their sockets. Lia screamed, her eyes wide with terror. Max held on with all his strength as he was wrenched downwards through the dark water. Jagged rocks whizzed past. The ship was plummeting. Lia struggled, trying to pull her leg free. Max's arms were burning and he could feel the water pressure crushing him.

"Rocks, Max!" Rivet cried from far above. Max heard a thundering rumble, and looked up to see an avalanche tumbling down the chasm wall, straight towards him. His heart lurched.

As Max clung desperately to the porthole, he could see Lia tugging and heaving at the chest, her face pale.

"Max, go!" she cried.

"I'm not leaving you!" Max shouted. But his fingers started to slip from the falling ship. "Lia!" Max cried as he finally lost his grip. The ship dropped away from him, hurtling downwards. The rumble of falling rocks was all around him. Max kicked his legs and swam as fast as he could away from the canyon wall.

He glanced over his shoulder to see the avalanche thunder past, filling the water with silt.

A hollow dread settled in the pit of his stomach. He forced himself to look down,

and saw the ship crash into the rocky canyon floor. A moment later a torrent of rocks smashed down on top of it.

For what seemed like a long time, the sound of thundering rocks and buckling metal filled Max's ears. Then finally, there was silence. Max stared downwards through clouds of swimming silt. He could see no sign of Lia. No sign of the ship at all.

CHAPTER NINE

THE TUSKED TERROR

Max gazed through clouds of billowing dust at the pile of rubble in the dark water below. He heard the whir of Rivet's propellers as the dogbot swam to his side.

"Where Lia, Max?" Rivet said. Max shook his head. He could feel his eyes prickling with tears.

Spike darted past. He started swimming in circles, glancing at the canyon floor. Max tried to swallow the tightness in his throat, but it was no good. Lia was gone.

Suddenly, Spike darted downwards through the cloudy water and started nosing at the rocks.

"No, Spike!" Max shouted.

But then he saw some of the smaller stones shifting. He felt a rush of hope and kicked his legs, forcing himself down through the deep water. He could see a pale webbed hand pushing through the rubble.

"Lia!" Max cried. He started shoving stones and rocks aside. Spike did the same, shovelling with his sword, and Rivet scrabbled with his front legs. Soon they had uncovered Lia's arm.

Max grabbed her hand and pulled as Rivet and Spike shifted more rocks. At last Lia slid from the hole they had made, and pushed her long hair away from her face.

"Phew!" she said. "That was horrible!" She

had a scratch on her forehead and a bruise on her arm, but other than that she was totally unharmed and smiling with relief.

"I thought you were dead!" Max said. "Even my sub would have been crushed under that lot." Lia tapped her chest, and Max saw she was wearing the Breastplate of Addulis.

"It channels the strength of the creatures of the deep," Lia said. "It can withstand any force."

Max looked at the silvery-grey stone with admiration. "I could make invincible tech with that!" he said.

Lia shook her head. "Only the Merryn can work stone like this," she said. "A Breather would never be able to do it. Even one with the Merryn Touch."

Brux's booming roar echoed down through the water. Max looked up and saw the creature's bloated, shining belly hovering far above them.

"Wait," Max said. "Maybe we can defeat Brux using the armour! If I put it on and lure him in, he'll try to crush me. Then you throw me the Spear, and I'll smash his controls from underneath."

Lia grinned. "Let's do it!" she said. She

shrugged the armour off, and passed it to Max. As Max lifted it over his head, he found that it was surprisingly light and comfortable.

Spike let out a series of warning clicks and Max glanced up to see Brux flick his tail towards a metal sub near the edge of the canyon. *THUD!* The blow sent it tumbling over the edge.

"Let's get out of here!" Max said. He grabbed onto Rivet's back legs as Lia leaped onto Spike's back.

Spike zoomed upwards and Rivet whizzed after him, his engines throbbing. Black shapes of falling rocks and chunks of metal filled the water as Brux swiped more wreckage into the canyon. Spike and Rivet dodged between them.

Brux's huge form loomed closer and closer. Max felt a twinge of fear at the thought of being trapped under its massive belly, but he shrugged it off. *There's no other way.*

"I'm going in!" he shouted to Lia. "Get into position." Lia threw him a thumbs-up, and Max released his grip on Rivet and swam up towards Brux. He darted past the colossal walrus, over the lip of the canyon and onto the ocean floor. As he did so, Brux's blunt nose shot up, and its black eyes swivelled towards Max.

"Over here, you big bag of blubber!" Max cried, lifting his hyperblade.

Brux flicked its massive tail and lunged towards him. Adrenaline surged through Max as the huge weight of metal and muscle cannoned towards him. The Robobeast reared up, lifting its bronze belly and throwing Max into shadow. Its glinting tusks were angled downwards towards Max. In the folds of thick skin near Brux's bristly mouth, Max could see the silver control box glinting.

Max glanced over his shoulder as Brux let out another roar. Lia was leaning out from behind a rock, holding the Pearl Spear of Addulis. Max could see Rivet and Spike behind her. *Perfect!*

He turned back to Brux just as the creature's roar rumbled into silence. Brux's dark eyes flashed, then its giant head and chest came crashing downwards. Max felt a jolt of terror. The curved point of a tusk was jabbing straight towards his face. Max gripped his hyperblade in both hands and swung it in a wide arc towards the falling tusk. Time seemed to slow. Max's blade flashed as it sliced the water.

CRASH! The blow connected, smashing the tusk sideways, but it left Max's arm ringing with pain. Brux lifted its head and brought it down again.

Max darted back out of reach. As Brux's

flat nose swept past him, Max lunged and sliced the tip of his blade across one tusk, leaving a gleaming mark in the metal.

"Come on!" Max shouted. "Is that the best you can do?"

Brux bellowed in rage. Its vast tail lifted and crashed against the ground, shaking

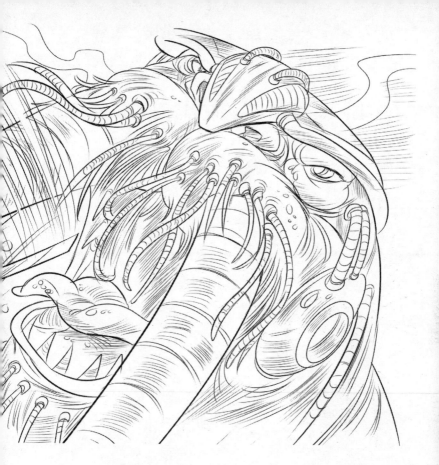

the ocean bed. Max's legs gave way and he
tumbled onto his back.

Max ignored the pain of the fall and the
thundering of his heart. He watched as Brux
powered towards him, swimming just above
the ocean floor. Soon a wall of scarred bronze
rose above him. *This is my chance!*

The Robobeast let out a bellow, then came crashing downwards.

"Now!" Max cried, glancing towards Lia's rock.

Lia lifted the Pearl Spear of Addulis, drew back her arm, and threw.

Max snatched the Spear from the water as it darted past his face. Then he braced himself as Brux's bronze belly fell towards him.

SMASH! The sound of metal crashing against stone was so loud that Max thought his eardrums might burst. He could feel the ground beneath his body shaking, the vibration running through his bones. The scratched and dented bronze of Brux's belly rested against his chest. But Max could barely even feel it. *The Breastplate works!*

Max looked up and saw Brux's whiskered head above him. Behind one tusk, he could see the silver control box. Brux's round eyes swivelled towards Max, then its long tusks came slicing downwards.

It's now or never…

CHAPTER TEN

SOMEBODY'S WATCHING

Max lifted the Pearl Spear high and swiped it through the air. The tip of the spear slid between the metal box and the creature's neck, just managing to slice it free. The box floated down towards Max, trailing silvery wires.

Brux froze, its sharp tusks hovering above Max's face. Then it slowly lifted its head and looked around. Max felt the creature's huge weight shift from his Breastplate. He kicked his legs and swam back out of range of the walrus's tusks.

Brux's large bronze bellyplate fell away, revealing wrinkled, blubbery flesh

underneath. The metal covering Brux's tusks tumbled off too. Its round eyes stared about, their whites showing in the gloom. Max felt a pang of pity. The giant sea creature looked terrified.

Lia swam towards Brux on Spike. She put her hand on the walrus's side and smiled up at him. Then she started to speak in a gentle, high-pitched whine. Brux blinked down at her, his eyes suddenly bright and full of intelligence.

Max saw Lia frown in concern. Soon her face darkened with anger. When Brux finally dropped its gaze, Lia stroked her hand along its massive neck and bowed her head. When she raised her eyes, they were filled with sadness.

Brux bowed its head to her in return, and then to Max. Then it turned and swam away.

Max swam to Lia's side, and Rivet whirred

over to join him. "What was that about?" Max asked.

"Red Eye – or should I say Siborg – grew that poor creature in a tank," Lia said angrily. "Brux never had any parents, or any of its own kind. It asked me to thank you for setting it free."

"It was grown in a tank?" Max said. He shook his head in disgust. "That's horrible. Siborg must be mixing robotics and genetics. Just like the Professor."

"Siborg is a monster!" Lia said, clenching her fist. "We have to stop him."

"He'll be after the next piece of battle-gear," Max said. "We'd better get back to the ship and beat him to it."

They swam back through the dark, oily water, filled with the hulks of sunken wrecks. Max kept a lookout for cyrates, but the sea was silent and still.

When they reached the ship, Lia slipped from Spike's back and put on her Amphibio mask. Together they climbed up the ship's ladder and onto the deck, Rivet trotting at their heels.

When they reached the bridge, Roger grinned. "I was just about to send out a rescue party," he said.

Grace rushed towards Max. "You did it!" she said. She put out a hand and touched the silver stone Breastplate Max was wearing. "Can I have a go?"

Max looked at Lia and raised an eyebrow. Lia nodded.

"I don't see why not," Max said. He took off the Breastplate, and Grace slipped it on. It came down to her knees, but Grace grinned and picked up her plastic blaster. She started racing about, firing shots at imaginary cyrates.

Rivet chased after her, barking and wagging his tail. Then suddenly the dogbot stopped and stood completely still, his ears pricked and his tail pointed. His eyes started to flash red.

"Greetings, vermin," Rivet barked.

Max felt his skin crawl. Whoever was

speaking, it wasn't Rivet.

Grace spun and aimed her plastic blaster at Rivet, and Lia and Roger both turned towards the dogbot, frowning.

"Ah! It seems I have your attention," Rivet went on in a flat monotone, his eyes flashing steadily. "My name is Siborg. You may know me by my barbaric alias, Red Eye." Lia drew a sharp breath, and Max felt a growing unease. "I have been watching you for some time," the chilling voice continued. "I could have killed you at any point, but I enjoy my games. And I must say, you've impressed me so far. As I suspected, your combination of tech and Merryn powers seems to be rather powerful. But your knowledge of technology is no match for mine. I disabled the Aquoran defence shields easily with my tech-disrupter device. You may recognise its effects, Max."

Max shivered at the sound of his name spoken in that cruel metallic voice. Then, with a jolt of horror, he realised what Siborg meant. *The hydrodisk!* The sub hadn't broken when Max had been surrounded by cyrates. Siborg must have powered it down with his tech-disrupter. He'd been close by the whole time!

"I have allowed you to collect two of the Arms of Addulis," Siborg continued. "But of course I shall be taking them back shortly. It's been interesting testing you, but now I find I have had enough. You can take this as a final warning. I have upgraded your status from potential threat to hostile force. Next time I see you, I will destroy you." Rivet's eyes blinked once more, then went dark.

Rivet shook himself all over, and looked at Max. "Game, Max?" Rivet said.

Max rushed over to the dogbot and flipped

open his control panel. Inside, he could see a strange, glassy-looking chip embedded in Rivet's circuits. *A bug!* Max used his fingernail to prise it out, then closed Rivet's controls.

"Rivet? Do you know how this got here?" Max asked, holding up the chip.

"No, Max," Rivet said. "Game, Max?"

Max shook his head, and patted Rivet's metal back. "Not now, Riv," he said.

"That was creepy!" Grace said, shivering.

"I wonder how long Siborg's been spying on us," Lia said.

"He must have installed the bug when we lost Rivet in that murky water," said Max. "When the cyrates ambushed us."

"He's been playing us for fools," Roger said.

"Well, if Red Eye thinks he can destroy us, he's got another think coming," Max said.

"We've beaten the Professor, and Cora. We can beat Red Eye too. Or Siborg, or whatever this twisted pirate wants to call himself. Full speed ahead, Roger!"

Just two more pieces of legendary battle-gear to find. Max only hoped that the mysterious Siborg didn't get them first.

Don't miss Max's next Sea Quest adventure,
when he faces

VENOR
THE SEA SCORPION

WIN AN EXCLUSIVE
GOODY BAG

In every Sea Quest book the Sea Quest logo is
hidden in one of the pictures. Find the logos in books
17-20, make a note of which pages they appear on and
go online to enter the competition at

www.seaquestbooks.co.uk

Each month we will put all of the correct entries into a draw
and select one winner to receive a special Sea Quest goody bag.

You can also send your entry on a postcard to:

Sea Quest Competition, Orchard Books,
338 Euston Road, London, NW1 3BH

Don't forget to include your name and address!

GOOD LUCK

Closing Date: 30th April 2015

DON'T MISS THE
BRAND NEW SERIES OF:

Series 15: VELMAL'S REVENGE

WARDOK
THE SKY TERROR

978 1 40833 487 4

XERIK
THE BONE CRUNCHER

978 1 40833 489 8

PLEXOR
THE RAGING REPTILE

978 1 40833 491 1

QUAGOS
THE ARMOURED BEETLE

978 1 40833 493 5

COMING SOON